TO LOGAN

First edition, August 2018.
ISBN 978-1-949543-00-1

BUDFORD & MOOSH
the great zoomy zoo caper

BY

SARA AND DAVID FURNAL

"WE'RE ABOUT TO LEAVE RIGHT NOW, HONEY" DADDY SAYS.

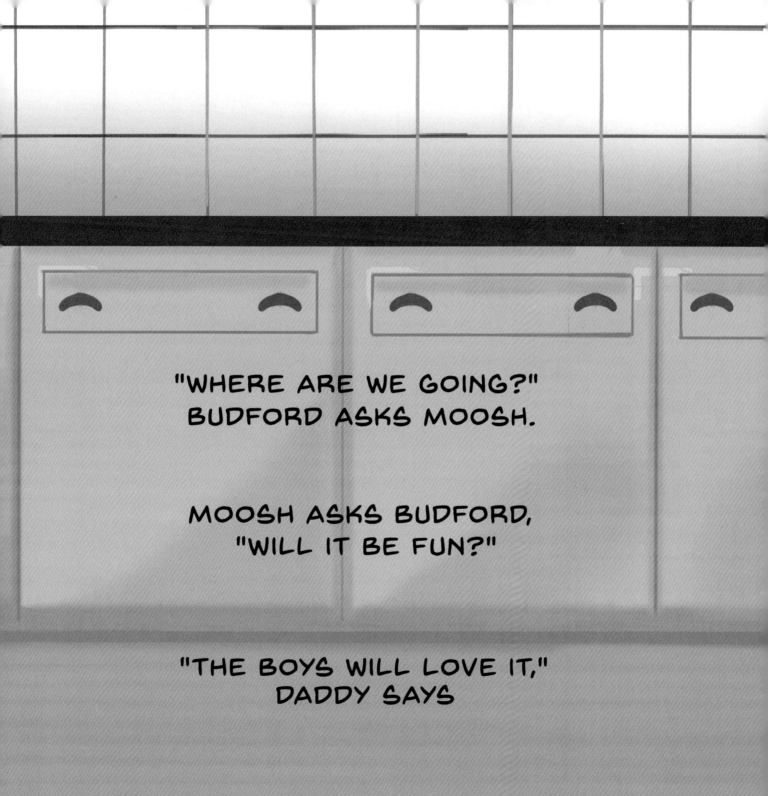

"I DON'T KNOW IF YOU'RE AWARE OF THIS,
DADDY, BUT I LOVE NUM NUMS,"
BUDFORD SAYS.

MOOSH NODS HIS HEAD IN AGREEMENT.

"I KNOW HOW MUCH YOU
BOYS LOVE YOUR FOOD."

THE PUPS DAYDREAM OF WATERMELON
AND GREEN BEANS AND PEANUTS.

"THE ZOO! WE'RE GOING
TO MAKE NEW ANIMAL FRIENDS!"

A FUZZY LITTLE CRITTER
RUNS UP TO DADDY.

HE MAKES FUNNY NOISES.

"BOYS, THIS IS MY FRIEND, HOWARD."

HOWARD JUMPS AND HOOTS.

THEN, SOMETHING AWFUL HAPPENS.

HE RUNS AWAY WITH THE PICNIC
BASKET FULL OF NUM NUMS!

"WAIT!"

"COME BACK, PLEASE!"

"BE CAREFUL WITH OUR SNACKS!"

HOWARD RACES FAR AHEAD.

"HE DROPPED OUR BAG OF
DELICIOUS PEANUTS, MOOSH!"

"MMM, PEANUTS!"

"FOCUS, MOOSH!
HE RAN INTO THE ANIMAL HABITATS!"

"I THINK HE WENT IN HERE, BROTHER."

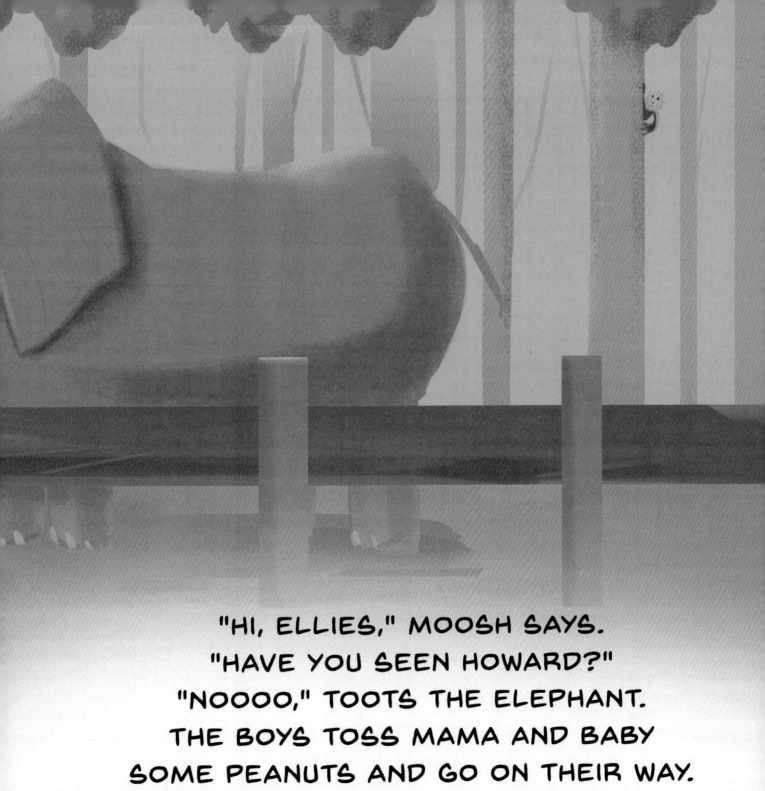

"HI, ELLIES," MOOSH SAYS.
"HAVE YOU SEEN HOWARD?"
"NOOOO," TOOTS THE ELEPHANT.
THE BOYS TOSS MAMA AND BABY
SOME PEANUTS AND GO ON THEIR WAY.

BUDFORD AND MOOSH RUN ACROSS A
SPECTACULAR PANDA FULL OF FLUFF.
"HAVE YOU SEEN A MONKEY
WITH A BASKET?"

"NO, LITTLE ONES. I HAVE NOT
SEEN ONE IN MY BAMBOO FOREST."
"I'M LOST!" MOOSH YELPS.
"COME ON, SILLY."

"AREN'T YOU SCARED
OF GETTING WET?"

"AU CONTRAIRE," MR. OTTER SAYS.
"I LOVE MY WATERY HOME."

"I DON'T THINK MONKEYS LIVE
IN WATER, BROTHER," BUDFORD SAYS.

"THE ONE YOU SEEK WENT THAT WAY,"
MR. OTTER POINTS WITH HIS TAIL.

"DO YOU THINK HE LOOKS LIKE ME?"
MOOSH ASKS BUDFORD
AS THEY TROT AWAY.

"OOOOH, ARE YOU A BIG KITTY?"
MOOSH ASKS.

"I AM NO KITTEN. I AM A TIGER."

"WOW," BUDFORD SAYS.
"HAVE YOU SEEN OUR PICNIC BASKET?
OR HOWARD?"

"I DO NOT CARE ABOUT
SUCH TRIVIAL THINGS.
I MUST SURVEY MY KINGDOM NOW."

MOOSH'S EARS FLOP IN DEFEAT.

"DON'T GIVE UP YET, MOOSH!"

"SSSSSSO, YOU ARE LOOKING FOR
THE MONKEY," SNAKE SAYS.

THE BOYS NOD AND WAG THEIR TAILS.

"HE WENT THAT WAY," IGUANA SAYS,
POINTING HIS NECK TO HIS LEFT.

"NO, I SSSSAW HIM GO THAT WAY,"
SNAKE SAYS, STICKING HIS
TONGUE STRAIGHT AHEAD.

"OH, NO! WHAT DO WE DO?"

"CHIN UP, MOOSH! WE'LL FIND A WAY!"

THE PUPS HEAR A MONKEY HOOT!

"I TOLD YOU, MOOSH! THERE HE IS!"

THEY FOLLOW HIM IN HOT PURSUIT.

"OUR FAMILY! HOWARD! ANIMALS! NUM NUMS! HOORAY!"

DRAW BUDFORD AND MOOSH!

JOIN US FOR MORE ZANY FUN IN THE ADVENTURES OF BUDFORD AND MOOSH SERIES!

BE PART OF THE PUPPY PACK! SIGN UP FOR THE MAILING LIST
AT WWW.BUDFORDANDMOOSH.COM.

SARA FURNAL IS A FREELANCE WRITER/EDITOR AND A PART-TIME COLLEGE PROFESSOR.
YOU CAN FIND HER ON TWITTER @SFURNAL.

DAVID FURNAL IS A GRADUATE IN ILLUSTRATION FROM ART CENTER COLLEGE OF DESIGN
IN PASADENA, CA. YOU CAN FIND HIM ON TWITTER @DFURNAL

SARA AND DAVID LOVE PLAYING FETCH WITH THEIR DOGS, WHO ARE THE INSPIRATION
FOR BUDFORD AND MOOSH, SPENDING TIME WITH THEIR FAMILY,
READING, GAMING, NAPPING, AND ALL THINGS NERDY.

Made in the USA
Lexington, KY
10 March 2019